Soft Lies
and
Wild Truths

A Poetic Journey Through Love, Heartbreak, and Self-Discovery

Liliana
Caliente-Cazadora

Soft Lies
and
Wild Truths

A Poetic Journey Through Love,
Heartbreak, and Self-Discovery

X

@CazadoraLiliana

author-liliana.com

Dedication

For the ones who stayed too long.
For the ones who believed when they shouldn't have had to.
For the ones who gave away their softness
to people who didn't know how to hold it.

And most of all—
for the ones who are still learning
that choosing yourself
is not a betrayal.
It's the beginning
of coming home.

With love,
Liliana

Author's Note

From Liliana Caliente-Cazadora

There are lies we tell others to protect them.
There are lies we tell ourselves to survive.
And then there are the ones we wrap in velvet—soft, beautiful, and almost believable.

This book is made of those lies.
And the wild, unruly truths that come after.

Soft Lies and Wild Truths is not just about love—it's about the illusions we fall into with open arms, and the brutal honesty that waits on the other side. It's about longing, betrayal, desire, silence, and the strength it takes to stand in the wreckage and choose yourself.

These poems are pieces of that journey. Some are whispers. Some are screams. All of them are true, even the ones that started out as lies.

If you've ever loved someone who didn't stay,
or believed in a future that never arrived,
or silenced your own needs just to be held—
this book is for you.

Thank you for holding my words.
I hope they hold you back.

With love and fire,
Liliana

Table of Contents

The First Lie: Hope

Velvet Promises

By Liliana Caliente-Cazadora

You said the night was made for us,
that the sky had waited its whole life
to wrap itself around our laughter.
And I believed you—
because I wanted to.
Because I needed something to believe in
more than I needed truth.

Your words came soft,
like velvet against the bruises
I pretended weren't there.
You spoke in futures—
not the kind that arrive,
but the kind that hover
just close enough to chase.

We lay in tangled sheets,
your voice dripping honey into my ears,
sweet lies I swallowed like prayer.
You called me your muse,
your miracle,
your reason to start again.

I memorized the script
you never had to write down.
I knew where to sigh,
when to nod,
how to become the woman
you needed me to be.

You never promised forever—
not exactly—
but you held me like someone
who believed in it,
and I mistook your arms for truth.

Some nights, I thought I saw it—
the flicker of something real
behind your eyes,
but it vanished
like the stars you said
were burning just for me.

You built a home with your hands,
but only in the dark,
where walls were shadows
and doors were never locked.
And when morning came,
it all faded,
like steam on a mirror.
Like a name never said aloud.

I should've asked more questions.
Should've noticed the way you blinked
when I said, *love*.
But I didn't—
because when velvet wraps around you,
you forget it's still a rope.

And even now,
with scars where your words used to rest,
I still remember the warmth.

The softness.
The way your lies felt
almost like love.

Painted in Moonlight
By Liliana Caliente-Cazadora

You told me the moonlight made everything softer—
my skin,
your breath,
the guilt in your voice.

And I believed it,
because I wanted to be something soft for once.
Something worthy of slow touches and quiet praise.

You painted me in silver,
your words like brushstrokes across my chest,
delicate, deliberate.
Every compliment a color.
Every sigh a frame.

I was a gallery you visited at night—
lingering,
admiring,
never staying.

You never said you loved me.
Not in words.
But you stared like I was a secret
you were afraid to keep
and even more afraid to lose.

You kissed like a man with memories to erase,
like you wanted to forget who you were
by drowning in who I could be.

We talked in whispers,
as if the daylight might hear
and ruin everything.

I memorized the shadows on your face,
thinking they were constellations,
mapping out a future
that only existed
in the space between
your heartbeat
and mine.

But moonlight is only silver
when you're not looking too closely.
It fades by morning.
So do men like you.

And still—
if you asked me to stand there again,
bathed in soft lies and silver light,
I might.
Just for one more painting
you'd never hang.

A Garden Without Thorns
By Liliana Caliente-Cazadora

You said I was safe with you.
That your heart was a garden,
and I could walk barefoot through it
without bleeding.

No thorns here,
you whispered—
just roses,
just sun.
Just hands that knew how to hold,
not hurt.

And I let myself bloom
in the warmth of those words.
I leaned into the breeze
of your affection,
let it carry me,
like petals caught in a summer wind.

You watered me with praise.
Fed me glances
that felt like miracles
when I'd only ever known drought.

You never rushed me.
Never raised your voice.
You smiled like sunlight
and touched me like rain—
soft, necessary,
just enough.

But something in me
knew gardens don't grow like this.
Not without roots.
Not without effort.
Not without a little pain.

Still, I wanted to believe.
I wanted to wake in a world
where love didn't bite
or bruise
or leave.

So I stepped deeper
into your garden,
ignoring the silence
where soil should've been.

I didn't see the absence as a warning.
I called it peace.

I didn't see the stillness as a lie.
I called it calm.

I didn't see you slipping away.
I only saw
roses
without thorns.

And maybe that was the cruelest lie of all—
to give me something beautiful
with nothing
to hold it
in place.

The Sound of Your Silence
By Liliana Caliente-Cazadora

It wasn't what you said
that made me fall.
It was what you didn't.

The silence between your sentences
was a warm place,
a quiet pocket
where I could rest my doubt.

You held my hand without pulling me close.
You kissed me like you were afraid
you'd forget how.
There was always a pause
before you answered,
like you were editing
before the truth could slip out.

But I didn't mind.
Not then.
I told myself it was mystery,
not avoidance.
Depth, not distance.

I was good at translating nothing
into something—
a shrug into affection,
a sigh into devotion.

I let your silence speak for you.
And I gave it the kindest voice I knew.

The way you looked away
when I asked what you wanted—
I called that shyness.
When you disappeared for days
and returned with tired eyes,
I called that life.

I filled the gaps in you
with all the pieces I hoped were real.
Built a man out of guesses
and fairy tales
and half-felt touches
that left fingerprints
on my soul.

You never lied.
Not exactly.
But you never told the truth either.
You just stayed quiet long enough
for me to write the story
I wanted to read.

And when it ended,
I couldn't say you broke me—
only that I broke myself
on the sound
of your silence.

The Second Lie: Forever

Blueprints for a Life
By Liliana Caliente-Cazadora

You spoke of a house with wide windows
and creaky floors
that would echo with laughter.
Of coffee in the mornings,
your arm around me,
the smell of something warm in the kitchen.

You didn't say *if.*
You said *when.*

And that's how I knew it was love.
Not the flowers.
Not the way your fingers tangled in mine.
But the way you made forever sound
like it already belonged to us.

We built a life in late-night talks—
a garden,
a dog,
a porch swing for two.
You told me what color you'd paint the walls
and asked what I'd name our first child.

I said I wasn't sure
if I even wanted children,
and you just smiled
and said, *Maybe you will. With me.*

You carved a future from smoke
and placed it in my hands

like it was real.
And I held it,
believing I could mold it into something solid
if I just loved you hard enough.

We made plans like blueprints—
clean lines,
measured corners,
a space for everything.
But we forgot to build
the foundation.

Forgot that someday
a storm might come
and test the walls.
Or maybe
you always knew
you wouldn't stay long enough
to see the roof go on.

Now, when I hear someone
talk about their forever,
I want to ask:
Is it real?
Or just something beautiful
you say to pass the time
between the lie
and the leaving?

Paper Rings and Midnight Wishes
By Liliana Caliente-Cazadora

You never gave me diamonds.
You twisted notebook paper into rings,
slipped them on my finger
like they meant something eternal.

"This is just until I can afford the real thing,"
you said,
but you looked at me like I already was
your always.
And that was enough.
God, it was enough.

We made vows under streetlamps,
not stars.
Lit candles on your nightstand
like altars
to a love we swore would last.

You made a toast with grape soda
and called it champagne,
and I laughed like it didn't matter—
because it didn't.
Not then.
Not when I had your eyes on me
like a secret promise.
Not when your voice
was still warm
with wanting me.

You made me believe
that real love didn't need gold,
or grand gestures,
or a witness.
Just two hearts
beating in the same direction.

And I carried that ring in my pocket
for months.
Even after it unraveled.
Even after you started leaving
before morning.

Because some part of me
still wanted to believe
that you meant it.
That maybe the paper
was just paper—
but the feeling
was something stronger.

We kissed on sidewalks,
talked about weddings
like they were fairy tales
we could write ourselves.

You said we didn't need permission
or a church
or anyone's blessing
but our own.

And I wanted that to be true—
wanted it more than I wanted

stability
or proof
or anything that could've saved us.

I still have that ring,
tucked inside a shoebox
with other soft lies
I once called love.
And sometimes,
late at night,
I wonder if you meant it—
even for a moment.

Because a wish whispered at midnight
can sound an awful lot
like a promise
when you want it badly enough.

Every Word You Never Meant
By Liliana Caliente-Cazadora

You said things
like you were sketching them in the air,
quick strokes,
easy to erase.
But I carved them into me—
every syllable,
a hope.
Every pause,
a place I filled with meaning.

You told me I was the calm in your chaos,
the lighthouse when you were drowning.
You said I saved you.
Over and over,
you said I saved you.

But what were you saving me from?

You never stayed long enough
to be the answer.
Just long enough to be the question
that kept me up at night.

There was a rhythm to your voice—
like a lullaby
meant to distract me
from the fact
that your arms were never rooted.
Always ready to reach
for something else.

I replay your words now
the way someone replays
an old voicemail—
the sound clear,
the meaning lost
in hindsight.

"I've never felt this way before."
"You're different."
"This scares me, too."

Back then,
those words were medicine.
Now, they taste like smoke.

You spoke in poetry,
but you never stayed for the ending.
You painted pictures
and left me to clean the brushes,
to hang the frames,
to explain to myself
why you weren't there
to see what we made.

And maybe the worst part
is that you never lied outright.
You let me believe
every word you didn't mean,
and I thanked you
for the silence
between your truths.

You said enough
to keep me close
but never enough
to keep me.

And I wonder now—
when you whispered those words,
did you know
they were only meant
to echo
in the empty room
you left behind?

The Weight of Maybe
By Liliana Caliente-Cazadora

You never said yes.
But you didn't say no either.
You lived in the pause,
in that breathless middle place
where hope blooms
and dies
in the same hour.

You told me
you "weren't ready"
but "could be someday."
And I clung to that someday
like it was a key,
like it unlocked something real
instead of leading me deeper
into rooms
you never meant to open.

You smiled when I dreamed aloud.
You didn't correct me
when I said *we*.
You let my voice shape a future
you never planned to enter.

And I convinced myself
that your silence was softness,
not hesitation.
That your distance

was patience,
not disinterest.

I built my life
in inches around you—
just enough space
for you to stay
if you ever decided to.

I told myself
maybe was kinder than no.
But maybe
is just a slow kind of goodbye.

The kind where you stay
long enough to haunt me.
Where I wake up wondering
if today is the day
you finally choose me—
not just for the night,
not just for the warm parts,
but for the hard ones, too.

You said you didn't want to hurt me.
That's why you never made promises.
But the truth is—
you did.

With every maybe.
With every almost.
With every look that said
not now,

but never quite said
never.

And I carried that weight
like it was love.
I carried it
until it crushed
the girl
who kept waiting
for yes.

The Cracks: Tiny Wild Truths

The Sigh Behind Your Smile
By Liliana Caliente-Cazadora

It was small at first—
a flicker,
barely a shift in your voice,
a breath that didn't quite land right.

You smiled,
but there was a sigh behind it.
The kind of sigh
you exhale when you're about to lie,
or leave,
or say something
you've already rehearsed.

I wanted to believe it was nothing.
A long day.
A missed call.
The weight of something
that had nothing to do with me.

But I knew.
Not in words.
Not in proof.
In that quiet way we know
when something we love
has already begun to disappear.

You touched me like you were memorizing
instead of staying.
Spoke softer,

as if your voice might wake the truth
you were trying to put back to sleep.

And I played along—
laughed at the right moments,
leaned into your shoulder
like it was still mine to lean on.

But there was a distance
in the way you blinked.
A shadow
you never let me chase.

And I wondered—
when did we stop being *we*
and start pretending?

You still told me I was beautiful,
but your eyes didn't hold it.
You still held my hand,
but your fingers no longer wrapped around mine
with the same knowing.

There is nothing louder
than a smile that doesn't reach the heart.
Nothing colder
than warmth given out of habit.

I wanted to ask—
but I didn't.
Because I was afraid
you'd answer.

And then everything
I tried not to see
would finally
become real.

Footsteps I Chose Not to Hear
By Liliana Caliente-Cazadora

You were leaving
long before the door closed.
Your body stayed,
but your spirit had already begun
its quiet retreat.

And I heard it.
I did.
In the way your voice changed
when you said my name—
softer,
like you were easing away
instead of reaching closer.

I felt the shift
in the way your hugs lost their hold,
how they became
a pause instead of a promise.

There were footsteps—
light ones,
cautious,
taken while I was looking the other way.

You tiptoed out of love
so carefully,
I almost believed
you were still with me.

But the signs were there.
In your late arrivals.
Your new silences.
The smile that took too long
to return.

I told myself
you were just tired.
That life had pulled you
in too many directions.
That I needed to be patient,
understanding,
better.

But the truth?
The truth had already started knocking.
I just refused to answer.

I made excuses
so I wouldn't have to ask the questions
that already had answers.
I wrapped your absence
in the fabric of hope,
wore it like a second skin,
even when it itched,
even when it burned.

You didn't hide your leaving.
I just didn't want to watch.

And maybe that's what hurts the most—
not that you left,
but that I helped you go

by pretending
you were still mine
long after
you weren't.

The Clock Ticked Louder at Night
By Liliana Caliente-Cazadora

The clock never used to bother me.
Its rhythm was background,
a heartbeat of the room,
steady, soft,
harmless.

But after you started pulling away,
it grew louder.
Sharper.
Each tick
a reminder that time was moving
and you were, too.

You would roll over
just out of reach.
Not enough to be cruel—
just enough to be gone.

I stopped sleeping first.
Started listening.
To the hum of absence,
to the ache in the quiet,
to the space between your breath
and mine.

You still kissed me goodnight,
but your lips felt like habit,
not hunger.
And your eyes didn't linger
when the lights went out.

So I counted seconds instead.
Listened to the ticking
like it might explain
what you wouldn't say.

Some nights,
I thought I heard you sigh—
not tired,
but trapped.
Like love had become
something to survive.

I should have asked you.
Should have turned on the light
and broken the silence.
But I was too afraid
your answer would echo
louder than the clock.
That once spoken,
truth would split the walls
we'd built from soft lies.

So I stayed still,
pretended sleep,
clung to your fading warmth
like it might remember
how to love me.

And the clock kept ticking.
Marking every moment
you were still here
but already gone.

Things You Didn't Say Out Loud
By Liliana Caliente-Cazadora

You never said you stopped loving me.
You didn't need to.

The words curled in the corner of your mouth,
waiting,
tamed by fear
or convenience
or maybe just cowardice.

But I heard them anyway.
In the way you hesitated
before coming home.
In the pauses that stretched too long
between questions
and answers.

You didn't say you were done trying—
but your effort grew thinner,
like the threadbare sweater
you used to drape around my shoulders
and stopped offering
when the nights got cold again.

You didn't say you were tired—
but your laughter had no echo.
Your smile, no heat.
And your touch
felt more like obligation
than devotion.

I searched for what you wouldn't say
in your patterns,
in the slope of your shoulders,
in the way your eyes scanned the room
without landing on me.

You spoke of work,
of errands,
of plans that didn't include "we"
as much as they used to.
I let it go.
Because I didn't want to be
the one to say it first.

You see,
I had my own words too—
things I buried
beneath "I'm fine"
and "maybe it's just a phase."

We both grew fluent
in silence.
Polite.
Measured.
Deadly.

And maybe love doesn't die
from one single blow—
maybe it fades,
slow and quiet,
while we both pretend

we don't notice the room
growing colder.

You didn't say goodbye.
But then again,
you didn't need to.
Some endings
announce themselves
without a sound.

The Shatter: Wild Truths Unleashed

You Were Always Leaving
By Liliana Caliente-Cazadora

The first time you left
was with your eyes.
They started drifting
when you thought I wasn't looking—
searching corners of the room
for exits
you hadn't taken yet.

You were there,
technically.
But only the body.
The rest of you
was already packing.

Your laugh left next.
It used to come so easily—
spilling from you
like light through open blinds.
But then it became quieter,
clipped,
as if joy had to be rationed
and I was no longer
worth the cost.

Your hands stopped lingering.
Your texts grew short.
Your kisses lost their timing—
just a second too fast,

too dry,
too forgettable.

And I kept telling myself
you were still mine.
That love had seasons.
That maybe this was winter
and spring would return
if I just held on.

But even in the holding,
I could feel the slipping.
Like trying to carry water
in cupped hands
that were already shaking.

You left in pieces.
A slow evacuation.
First your laughter.
Then your stories.
Then your desire
to know mine.

By the time your feet
crossed the doorway,
I had already said goodbye
a hundred silent times.

And maybe that's
what makes it so cruel—
you didn't break my heart
all at once.
You broke it slowly,

casually,
in moments I mistook
for distance,
not detachment.

You were always leaving.
I just took too long
to see it.

The Lie That Broke My Bones
By Liliana Caliente-Cazadora

It wasn't even a big one.
Not the kind that makes you scream,
or slam doors,
or burn old letters in the sink.

It was small.
Almost quiet.
A simple sentence
delivered like a shrug,
as if it didn't carry weight—
but it did.

God, it did.

It hit something inside me
I didn't know could shatter.
A place deeper than my heart.
Older than my trust.

It wasn't about what you did.
Not really.
It was about the moment I realized
you could look me in the eye
and say something
you knew wasn't true—
and still sleep that night.

That's what broke me.

The ease of it.
The calm in your voice
while my whole body braced
for a blow
I didn't even see coming.

I tried to stand still.
Tried to tell myself
it was just one crack,
a fracture we could heal.
But the truth?
That lie was the last thread
holding me upright.

And when it snapped,
I fell apart
in ways I didn't know were possible.

Bones remember
the weight of betrayal.
Skin remembers
the hands that trembled
before letting go.

You said,
"I didn't mean to hurt you."
As if intention
was some kind of bandage.

But pain doesn't care
why it was delivered.
It only knows
it was.

And now,
every part of me aches
with the knowledge
that love isn't always
what it claims to be.
Sometimes,
it's just the story we tell
until the truth is too loud
to ignore.

Ashes in the Shape of You
By Liliana Caliente-Cazadora

After everything,
you're still here.
Not in the way I hoped—
not in breath, or warmth, or voice—
but in the spaces
where you once were.

You exist now
in the scent of rain on pavement,
in the pause before a song begins,
in the places my fingers twitch to reach
before they remember
there's no one left to touch.

You burned through me
like wildfire—
bright, consuming,
beautiful in the worst possible way.

And now all that's left
is ash.

But somehow,
even that holds your shape.

The way you used to sit beside me,
legs slightly angled,
your hand resting on the table
but never quite reaching mine.
The way your eyes softened

when I laughed,
even when your heart
was elsewhere.

These fragments don't hurt
the way they used to.
Now they just echo.
Soft.
Haunting.
Familiar.

I've swept you from the corners,
washed the sheets,
boxed the photos—
but you linger
in the outline of everything I tried to rebuild.

I tell myself
it wasn't all lies.
That some part of you
meant to love me,
even if it couldn't last.

Maybe that's what hurts most—
the almost.
The shadow
of what could have been
if either of us had known
how to hold it right.

I am not angry anymore.
Just tired.
Just hollow

in the places
you once filled with dreams.

And though I've stopped searching,
I still carry you—
not as a flame,
but as dust.

Ashes
in the shape of you.

The Reckoning: The Wildness Within

What I Refused to See
By Liliana Caliente-Cazadora

It wasn't that I didn't know.
It was that I didn't want to.

I saw the signs—
the deflection in your smile,
the way you said my name
like it was something you were already forgetting.
But I wrapped those truths
in prettier lies,
and called them love.

I told myself
you were just afraid of being hurt,
that your distance was caution,
not cruelty.
That I could be patient enough,
good enough,
gentle enough
to make you stay.

I ignored the way you flinched
at vulnerability,
how your words became riddles
I kept solving
just to feel close to you.

I became fluent
in your excuses.
Read silence
like scripture.

Translated your detachment
into mystery,
like that made it beautiful.

But the truth was never hiding.
It was right there,
in the way I cried alone
and called it strength.
In the way I gave you
the best of me
while you rationed out
the bare minimum.

I let myself believe
that scraps were a feast.
That longing
was love.
That waiting
was loyalty.

But deep down,
I knew.
I knew from the moment
you kissed me
without meeting my eyes.

And still,
I stayed.
Not because I didn't see it—
but because I was too afraid
of what it meant
to finally look.

Now,
when I turn inward,
I don't ask why you did what you did.
I ask why I let you.

And the answer is simple.
I was taught to love
even when it hurts.
I was taught to endure
and call it devotion.

But not anymore.
Not again.

Now I see.
And this time,
I won't look away.

Love Isn't a Cage
By Liliana Caliente-Cazadora

I used to think
love meant sacrifice.
That bending myself into quieter shapes
was noble,
that staying silent
was strength.

I made myself small
so you could feel big.
Folded my edges
to fit the frame you built
from your own insecurities.

You never asked me to be less.
Not with words.
But your actions
shaped the walls just the same.
A look.
A sigh.
A laugh that told me
I'd gone too far
by simply being myself.

And I obeyed.
God, I obeyed.
Called it compromise.
Called it care.
Called it love.

But love doesn't ask you
to clip your wings
to stay close.
Love doesn't tremble
at your brightness
or build a cage
and call it protection.

I was not a bird.
But I learned to perch.
To sing softly.
To be grateful
for the bars.

Until one day
I woke up
and didn't recognize my voice.
Didn't know
what I wanted anymore.
Only what you liked.
What made you stay.
What didn't make you flinch.

That's not love.
That's containment.
And I want more than survival.
I want wildness.
I want a voice that echoes.
A presence that fills the room
without apology.

If you need me to shrink
to love me,
you don't love me.

And I won't stay
in a place
where freedom is treated
like a threat.

Love isn't a cage.
And I was never meant
to live behind bars.

How I Betrayed Myself
By Liliana Caliente-Cazadora

I thought the worst thing
was being left.
But it wasn't.
The worst thing
was watching myself stay
long after I knew
I deserved to go.

I betrayed myself
with every second chance
I handed you
like broken glass
I kept hoping wouldn't cut this time.

I betrayed myself
when I smiled through the silence,
when I dimmed my joy
because yours had gone out.

I called it loyalty.
But it was fear.
Fear of being alone.
Fear of starting over.
Fear that if I walked away,
I'd never be loved again.

So I gave you the softest parts of me,
even when you stopped asking.
Even when you stopped noticing.
And I told myself

that was strength.
That was commitment.

But what is love
if it costs you
your voice?
Your boundaries?
Your self?

I bent my spine
until it forgot how to stand.
Muted my instincts,
my needs,
the parts of me that whispered,
This isn't enough.

And when they screamed,
I still didn't listen.

I kept showing up
to a version of love
that never showed up for me.

I kept hoping
if I stayed long enough,
you'd see me.
Really see me.

But I was the one
who refused to look.
At the mirror.
At the truth.
At the aching girl

who just wanted
to be chosen
by someone
other than herself.

It's taken time—
but I'm learning now
that healing begins
not with blame,
but with forgiveness.
Not for you.
For me.

For every time I said yes
when I meant no.
For every time I stayed
when I wanted to run.
For every time I gave
when I was already empty.

I betrayed myself
in the name of love.

But I won't do it again.

The Freedom: Love Without Lies

Roots Before Roses
By Liliana Caliente-Cazadora

This time,
I plant the roots first.

No more rushing toward romance
like it's salvation.
No more climbing trellises made of red flags
because they looked like passion
in the dark.

I've learned
that love without foundation
is just a storm
waiting to happen.

So I'm digging deep now—
into the soil of my own becoming,
into the parts of me
I used to bury
to make space for someone else.

I no longer bloom
for another's gaze.
I bloom
because it's who I am.

I've spent too long
decorating empty soil,
faking spring
when my roots were starving.

No more.

This time,
I build something beneath the surface.
Boundaries like bedrock.
Honesty like water.
Kindness like sun.
Silence that heals,
not hides.

If love comes again—
and maybe it will—
it won't be the kind
that knocks me over.
It'll be the kind
that meets me in the garden
I made myself.
Not to take.
Not to tame.
But to walk beside me,
hands dirty with the same good work.

Because I've learned—
roses are beautiful,
but they mean nothing
if there's no root to hold them.

And I've finally stopped
mistaking petals
for promises.

The Fierce Bloom of Me
By Liliana Caliente-Cazadora

You thought you buried me.
Left me beneath the weight
of half-spoken truths,
slow goodbyes,
and the echo of your fading hands.

But I was never gone.
Only resting.
Only waiting
for the right season
to bloom again—
not for you,
but for me.

There is something sacred
in the breaking.
A clarity that rises
from the ruins.
Pain,
sharpened into purpose.

I have walked through fire
and now carry smoke
in my lungs
like a hymn.

I no longer dress my wounds
for your comfort.
No longer rewrite my story
to keep your name in it.

You were a chapter.
Not the whole book.
A lesson.
Not the definition
of my worth.

The soil you left me in
was bitter,
but still—
I grew.
Twisting toward the light
that was always mine,
even when I forgot.

I am not soft petals
wilting for your return.
I am thorns.
Roots.
A wild bloom
that refuses to apologize
for its color,
its reach,
its refusal to be held
without care.

You do not get to touch
what you once abandoned.
You do not get to taste
the fruit of my healing.

This garden
is mine now.

And I bloom
not to be admired,
but because I can.
Because I must.
Because even broken things
can blossom
with enough sun,
enough time,
and the decision
to rise.

Soft Hands, Sharp Edges
By Liliana Caliente-Cazadora

I used to think
I had to choose—
to be soft
or strong.
To love with open hands
or protect with closed fists.

But I've learned
I can be both.
I can hold you gently
and still know when to let go.
I can offer warmth
without setting myself on fire
to keep you from feeling cold.

This version of me
has soft hands—
but don't mistake that softness
for surrender.
I've walked through storms
with my palms open
and came out carrying myself.

I love deeply.
Still.
Always.
But not blindly.

Now, when I say *yes,*
it's because I mean it—
not because I'm afraid to say *no.*

I speak with grace
but draw my lines in ink.
I forgive
but don't forget
what I had to climb out of.

And I will not shrink
just to be more palatable.
Not again.
Not ever.

If you want to be close to me,
you'll have to learn
how to hold something
that shines and cuts
at the same time.

Because I am done
trimming my edges
to keep others comfortable.
I am done
bleeding quietly.

This love I give now
is honest.
Messy.
Brave.

It comes with softness—
yes.
But also
a fire I no longer fear.
A sharpness I've earned.

So if you love me,
love all of me.
The comfort
and the chaos.
The tenderness
and the steel.

Because I am not either/or.
I am soft hands,
sharp edges,
and the truth
I never learned to speak
until now.

This Time, I Choose Me
By Liliana Caliente-Cazadora

I used to believe
love was something to earn.
Something I had to chase,
prove,
hold together with both hands
even when it splintered.

I thought choosing someone else
meant I was good,
kind,
worthy.
That sacrifice was the price of staying.

But I've paid that price.
Again
and again.
And all it gave me
was silence,
regret,
and a hundred versions of myself
I didn't recognize.

So now—
I choose differently.

I choose peace
over potential.
Truth
over pretending.
I choose joy

that doesn't ask me to shrink,
and love
that doesn't require
I bleed quietly
to be kept.

This time,
I will not beg
for crumbs and call them comfort.
I will not twist myself
into softer shapes
to be less threatening.
I will not trade my voice
for a temporary place
in someone else's arms.

This time,
I choose the woman
who stayed up late
with her own heart.
Who gathered her broken pieces
and called them sacred.
Who learned how to bloom
without an audience.

I choose her.

I choose mornings without tension,
nights without fear,
and a heart that beats
because it is free—

not because it's chasing
what it was never meant to catch.

And if love finds me again,
it will be one that walks beside me,
not ahead,
not behind—
but with.

But whether it does
or it doesn't,
I am whole.

I am enough.

And for the first time in my life,
that is more than enough.

This time,
I choose me.

Closing Note

From Liliana Caliente-Cazadora

If you've made it this far, thank you.

Thank you for walking through the fire with me.
Through the hope and the heartbreak.
Through the soft lies I once believed
and the wild truths I had to learn the hard way.

This book was not easy to write.
It came from pieces of me I've often tried to hide—
the parts that stayed too long,
that loved too hard,
that hurt in silence
and called it strength.

But somewhere in the middle of all that ache,
something powerful began to grow.
Not bitterness—
but clarity.
Not revenge—
but return.
Not fear—
but freedom.

This isn't a story about being broken.
It's a story about coming back to myself.

If you see yourself in these pages—
if you've ever stayed when you should have left,
given more than you had to give,
or wondered if you were ever truly seen—

please know:
you are not alone.

And you don't have to keep choosing pain
just to feel loved.

You are worthy of peace,
of joy,
of a love that doesn't ask you to shrink.

And if no one has told you this lately—
you are enough.
Right now.
As you are.

I hope you carry that truth with you
like a flame.

With all my heart,
thank you for holding these poems.
And thank you
for holding me.

With love,
Liliana

About The Author

Liliana Caliente-Cazadora is a Latina author whose work explores the quiet ache of longing, the beauty of vulnerability, and the spaces between what's said and what's left behind. Born and raised in East Los Angeles, Liliana grew up surrounded by stories—spoken, whispered, and imagined—that continue to shape her voice today.

Known initially for her bold and sensual storytelling, Liliana has shifted toward more reflective and emotionally layered work, including poetry, romantic fiction, and literary pieces that honor the complexities of love, loss, and healing. Her writing blends raw honesty with lyrical tenderness, drawing readers into the kind of truths we rarely say out loud.

Now based in Denver, Colorado, she finds inspiration in mountain sunrises, local cafés, and the deep, transformative power of human connection. When she's not writing, she's reading romance novels, collecting notebooks she may never use, and occasionally texting things she'll never send.

www.ingramcontent.com/pod-product-compliance
Lightning Source LLC
Chambersburg PA
CBHW050831180626
46814CB00004B/1572